DIG!

Andrea Zimmerman
and David Clemesha

Illustrated by
Marc Rosenthal

Silver Whistle • Harcourt, Inc.

Orlando   Austin   New York   San Diego   Toronto   London

Library of Congress Cataloging-in-Publication Data
Zimmerman, Andrea Griffing.
Dig!/Andrea Zimmerman and David Clemesha; illustrated by Marc Rosenthal.
p. cm.
"Silver Whistle."
Summary: Follows Mr. Rally and his dog, Lightning, as they travel the town
on a big yellow digging machine, taking care of five important jobs.
[1. Excavating machinery—Fiction. 2. Construction workers—Fiction. 3. Dogs—Fiction.]
I. Clemesha, David. II. Rosenthal, Marc, 1949- ill. III. Title.
PZ7.Z618Di 2004
[E]—dc21   2003004373
ISBN 0-15-216785-4

First edition

A C E G H F D B

Printed in Singapore

The illustrations in this book were done in ink, watercolor, and Prismacolor pencil on watercolor paper.
The display lettering was created by Marc Rosenthal.
The text type was set in Elroy.
Color separations by Bright Arts Ltd., Hong Kong
Printed and bound by Tien Wah Press, Singapore
This book was printed on totally chlorine-free Stora Enso Matte paper.
Production supervision by Sandra Grebenar and Pascha Gerlinger
Designed by Linda Lockowitz

For Chase
—A. Z. & D. C.

To Willem
—M. R.

Mr. Rally drives a big yellow backhoe.

It has a scooper and a pusher.

Mr. Rally loves to dig in the dirt.

So does his dog, Lightning!

Mr. Rally
buckles his
overalls and
pulls on his
boots.

He has five big
digging jobs
to do today.

He counts them.

One.

Two.

Three.

Four.

Five.

JOBS
1
2
3
4
5

Job #1 up ahead.
One is a bridge on the ridge.

Mr. Rally drives up the ridge of the mountain.
Construction workers need Mr. Rally to move
dirt and rocks.

Dig up rock and dig up clay!
Dig up dirt and dig all day!

Good job, Mr. Rally!
Good job, Lightning!
Mr. Rally waves good-bye.

Is all the digging done? No!

Job #2 up ahead.
Two is a drain for the rain.

Mr. Rally drives to the new neighborhood in town.
Construction workers need Mr. Rally to shape the hill.

Dig up rock and dig up clay!
Dig up dirt and dig all day!

Good job, Mr. Rally!
Good job, Lightning!
Mr. Rally waves good-bye.

Is all the digging done? No!

Job #3 up ahead.

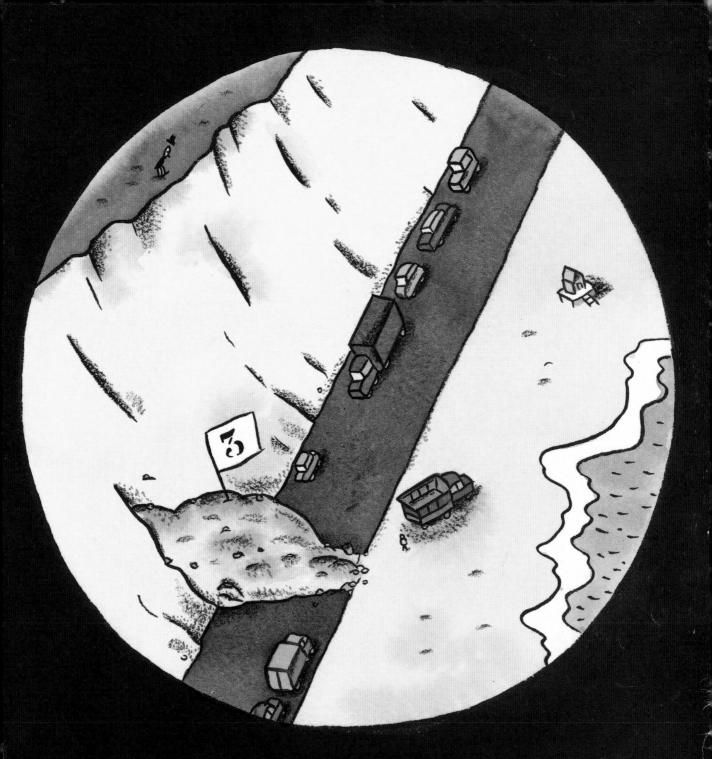

Three is a load on the road.

Mr. Rally drives to the ocean.
Construction workers need Mr. Rally to clear the landslide.

Dig up rock and dig up clay!
Dig up dirt and dig all day!

Good job, Mr. Rally!
Good job, Lightning!
Mr. Rally waves good-bye.

Is all the digging done? No!

Job #**4** up ahead.

Four is a pool at the school.

Mr. Rally drives past the playground.

Construction workers need Mr. Rally to dig the hole.

Dig up rock and dig up clay!
Dig up dirt and dig all day!

Good job, Mr. Rally!
Good job, Lightning!
Mr. Rally waves good-bye.

Is all the digging done? No!

Job #5 up ahead.
Five is a zoo, all brand-new.

Mr. Rally drives past the animals.
Construction workers need him to level the site.

Dig up rock and dig up clay!
Dig up dirt and dig all day!

Good job, Mr. Rally!
Good job, Lightning!
Mr. Rally waves good-bye.

Is all the digging done?

YES! Mr. Rally counts his jobs.

One, two, three, four, five.

One was the
bridge on the ridge.

Two was the
drain for the rain.

Three was the
load on the road.

Four was the
pool at the school.

Five was the
zoo, all brand-new.

All five jobs are finished. Whew! What a day!

The construction sites are closed now.
Mr. Rally drives his big backhoe home.

But Mr. Rally doesn't unbuckle his overalls.
He doesn't pull off his boots.

He says, "I dig up rock! I dig up clay!
I dig up dirt for work and play!"
Mr. Rally and Lightning have lots more digging to do . . .

. . . in their garden!

Good job, Mr. Rally! Good job, Lightning!